Hoppity Gets Lost

by Jane Carruth   illustrated by Tony Hutchings

MODERN PUBLISHING
A Division of Unisystems, Inc.
New York, New York 10022

Hoppity liked riding in Mr. Weasel's old bus. He enjoyed going to the stores with Mommy and Tufty. This morning the line was longer than ever and everyone was carrying their biggest shopping bag. Hoppity wished he had one too.

"Keep tight hold of Tufty," Mommy said, when it was time to get on the bus. "I do hope the big sale at the Department Store hasn't started." Hoppity was too excited to reply. He knew where he wanted to go when he got to the store.

The bus stopped near a huge store. Hoppity gasped when he saw the Woodville Bandsmen. They were blowing trumpets, banging drums, and clashing cymbals.

"I'll join the band when I'm big," Hoppity shouted above the noise. "I'll be a cymbal-clasher!"

"You'll be a good boy," said Mommy sharply. "And stay close to me. We must get to the Shoe Department and start looking for a sale on slippers. It's Daddy's birthday tomorrow."

"We're in luck," Mommy whispered to Hoppity when they were in the Shoe Department. "Everybody else has rushed to the coats."

The pretty salesperson brought out all kinds of slippers and Hoppity began to wish Mommy would decide. He looked around for something to do and saw an enormous pair of men's boots on the floor. Hoppity smiled broadly as he stuck his feet into the giant boots. At first Mommy was cross. But when she saw the smile on the salesperson's face, she smiled too.

Mommy got some new handkerchiefs for Hoppity and his brother Bobtail. Then she said, "How about some milk?"

"No thank you," said Hoppity firmly. "I want to go to the toys. So does Tufty. He wants to see all his bear cousins and I told him he could!"

"We'll have to use the elevator," Mommy said with a sigh.

Hoppity felt a bit scared inside the elevator, but the elevator operator just smiled and said, ''Going up! Which floor, please?''

Hoppity said loudly, ''Toys, please!''

Once inside the toy department, Hoppity ran straight for the shelves of small bears. "Look, Tufty!" he said. "Here are some of your cousins!"

Mommy waited patiently until Tufty had been properly introduced to his bear cousins. Then she said, "That's enough. Be a good boy, Hoppity, and leave the bears. You can have just one ride in the racing car."

Hoppity fit perfectly in the racing car. With his feet on the pedals and his hands on the steering wheel, he felt like a professional racing-car driver.

"I won't be a cymbal-clasher when I'm big," he cried. "I'll be a racing-car driver!"

"We'll see," said Mommy. "Climb out now!"

As they were leaving the Toy Department, Hoppity was
given a big yellow balloon. Before he could thank the kind
lady, a voice, as if from nowhere, boomed out, ''Special
sale on hats and bonnets on the first floor!''

The voice made Hoppity jump. ''Where is it?'' he
whispered. ''I can't see where it's coming from!''

''From that loudspeaker on the wall,'' said Mommy.

Hoppity was still thinking about the magic voice when Mommy went up to the hat counter. Then she met one of her friends and they were soon picking up and trying on bonnets. In the excitement of finding a bargain, she forgot about Hoppity, and soon he wandered away.

"It's time I found something to buy for you, Tufty," he said. And he went over to a basket filled with bright knitted hats and scarves. But finding a hat that fit Tufty's small head was not easy. Hoppity soon began talking just like his mother. "No, not that one—it doesn't suit you . . ." Then something dreadful happened. His beautiful new balloon was suddenly floating away. "Help! Help! Catch it, somebody!" he screamed.

Tufty's present was forgotten as Hoppity chased after the balloon. Soon he was caught up in a crowd of eager shoppers. Then he was swept away. The balloon was lost! Hoppity was lost! And he began to cry. After what seemed like hours, he found himself back in the Shoe Department. "I'm l-lost!" Hoppity sobbed, when the pretty salesperson came up to him. "I've lost M-Mommy!"

"Don't cry," said the pretty lady, as she helped Hoppity
blow his nose on his new handkerchief. "We can find lost
Mommies. But first I'll take you to the manager's office."

"My balloon is lost too," Hoppity whispered.

"We'll be happy to find you another one," said the lady.

When the manager told Hoppity he would call his mother over the loudspeaker, Hoppity began to smile. "You must be the magic voice," he said.

"That's right," said the manager. "It's the magic voice that finds lost Mommies." And soon—there was Mommy, very pretty in her new bonnet, hugging and kissing him.

"Why don't you leave Hoppity with us," said the manager, "while you finish shopping?"

Mommy looked doubtful. But then the door opened and
in came two more, tearful children. "Don't worry about
me," said Hoppity. "I'll tell them all about the magic voice
that finds lost Mommies and Daddies."
No wonder Mommy looked so proud as she hurried off!

When they were home again, Mommy went to the mirror to admire her new bonnet. Hoppity showed Daddy his new balloon and Tufty's new hat and all the presents—except the slippers hidden behind the cushion. But most of all he enjoyed telling him about the magic voice that found lost Mommies!